EEK!
Stories to make you shriek™

For Beginning Readers
Ages 6-8

This series of spooky stories has been created especially for beginning readers—children in first and second grades who are developing their reading skills.

How do these books help children learn to read?

- Kids love creepy stories and these stories are true page-turners (but never too scary).
- The sentences are short.
- The words are simple and repeated often in the story.
- The type is large with lots of room between words and lines.
- Full-color pictures on every page act as visual "clues" to help children figure out the words on the page.

Once children have read one story, they'll be asking for more!

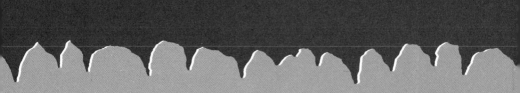

For Alexander Cook—K.McM.

To my parents—J.S.

Text copyright © 1996 by Kate McMullan. Illustrations copyright © 1996 by Jeff Spackman.
All rights reserved. Published by Grosset & Dunlap, Inc., which is a member of The Putnam &
Grosset Group, New York. EEK! STORIES TO MAKE YOU SHRIEK is a trademark of The
Putnam & Grosset Group. GROSSET & DUNLAP is a trademark of Grosset & Dunlap, Inc.
Published simultaneously in Canada. Printed in the U.S.A.

Library of Congress Cataloging-in-Publication Data

McMullan, Kate.
    The mummy's gold / by Kate McMullan ; illustrated by
Jeff Spackman.
        p.   cm. — (Eek! Stories to make you shriek)
    Summary: Jake thinks that the mummy he meets at a movie theater is
part of one of his brother's tricks, but he is wrong.
    [1. Mummies—Fiction. 2. Brothers—Fiction. 3. Horror stories.]
I. Spackman, Jeff, ill. II. Title. III. Series.
PZ7.M47879Mu   1996
[Fic]—dc20   95-46794
                                                                                   CIP
ISBN 0-448-41345-0 (GB)   A B C D E F G H I J   AC
ISBN 0-448-41310-8 (pb)   A B C D E F G H I J

asy-to-Read
ges 6-8

EEK!

Stories to make you shriek™

The Mummy's Gold

By Kate McMullan

Illustrated by Jeff Spackman

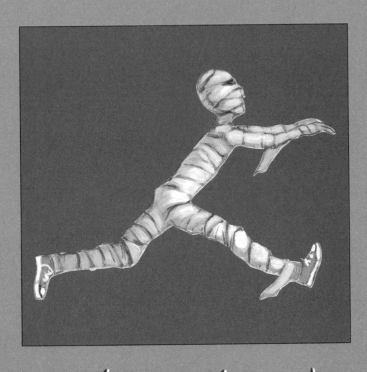

Grosset & Dunlap ● New York

My big brother, Henry,

likes to trick me out of my money.

One time, when I was little, Henry said,

"Hey, Jake! A nickel is bigger than a dime.

Right?"

Then he got me to give him

all my <u>little</u> dimes.

And he gave me his <u>big</u> nickels.

What a dirty trick!

Now I keep my money in my bank.

I have lots of money.

And I make sure that Henry

can't get his hands on it.

Last Saturday Henry said,

"Hey, Jake!

Max and I are going to a movie.

Want to come?

I will pay for you."

I was so surprised.

Right away I said, "Okay!"

But then I started to wonder.

Why was Henry paying for me?

What was he up to?

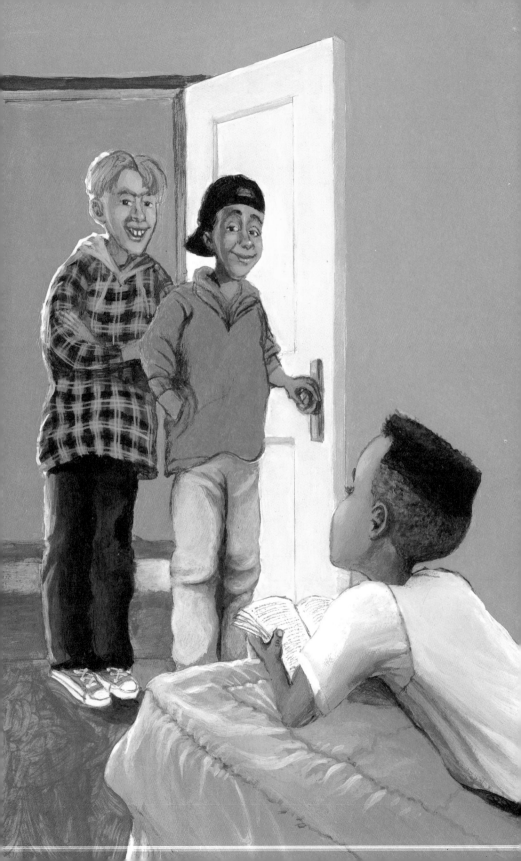

We got to the theater just in time. The movie was called "The Mummy's Gold."

In the movie,

a man with evil eyes found a tomb.

In the tomb was a mummy.

All at once the mummy sat up.

Right in his coffin!

The mummy's bandages were coming off.

Underneath was his 3,000-year-old skin.

Yuck!

I was scared.

I looked over at Henry.

He and Max were whispering.

Max pointed at me.

Then they started laughing.

Henry whispered, "Hey, Jake!

Lucky there aren't

any real <u>live</u> mummies!"

I nodded.

I nibbled on my popcorn.

And I wondered why Henry said that.

What were Max and Henry up to?

In the movie, the evil man stole

the mummy's gold. He hid it.

The mummy chased the evil man

all over the world.

Finally the mummy got him.

He grabbed him by the neck.

Slowly, he squeezed until

the man's evil eyes popped out!

Splat!

Then the mummy's face

on the screen grew bigger and bigger.

He seemed to be looking right at me!

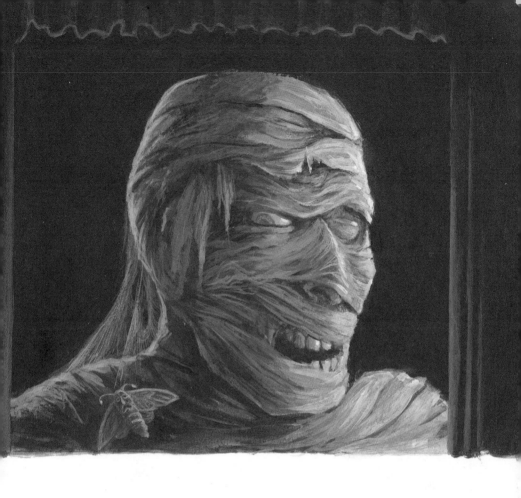

He said,

"I WANT MY GOLD!
I WILL SEARCH
UNTIL I FIND IT!"

Oh, man! I was shaking!

The movie seemed so real.

After the movie,

I followed Henry and Max outside.

It was almost dark.

For once I was glad Henry was around.

But he wasn't around for long.

"Hey, Jake!" he called. "See you!"

Then Henry ran off with Max.

What a rat!

I walked home by myself.

It was scary.

I tried not to think about that mummy.

I was almost home,

when I got a strange feeling.

Was somebody following me?

I slowly turned my head to see.

The street was empty.

I kept on walking.

But the strange feeling did not go away.

I started walking faster.

Then I heard something behind me.

Was it footsteps?

I spun around.

I could not believe my eyes!

At the corner stood . . .

No, it couldn't be!

But it was!

It was a mummy!

And it was coming closer.

I was so scared I could not move!

Then the mummy spoke.

"I WANT MY GOLD!" it wailed.

Just like in the movie!

I turned and ran.

I heard the mummy behind me.

I ran some more.

I zoomed up my front steps.

I stood there panting.

I saw the mummy walk away.

Then I saw something else.

The mummy had on a blue shirt!

The mummy was Henry!

I went inside.

Our parents were out.

So I stuck a pizza in the microwave.

Then I waited for Henry.

At last he came home.

"Why did you dress up like a mummy?"

I asked him.

"Why did you try to scare me?"

"I didn't!" Henry said.

But I knew better.

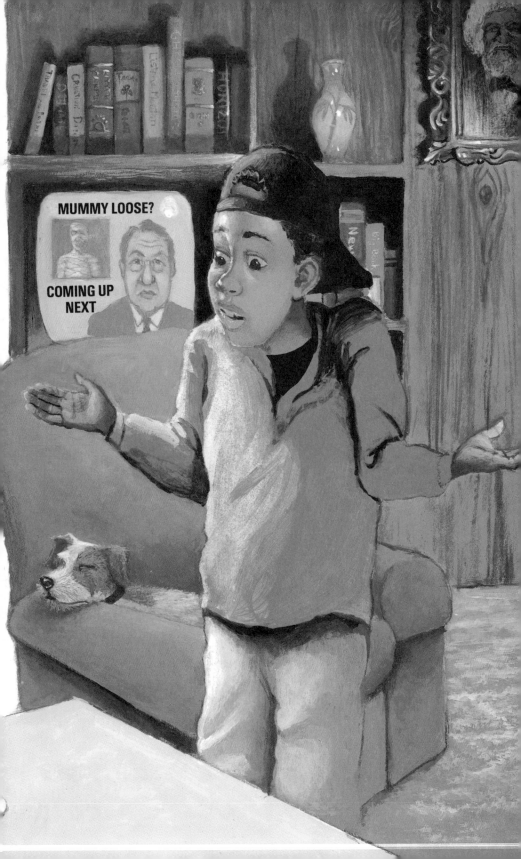

Later I put on my pj's and got into bed.

As I lay there,

I thought about getting back at Henry.

But then I heard a voice—

a voice from outside.

"I WANT MY GOLD!" it wailed.

I rushed to my window.

There was the mummy again!

But I was not scared now.

"Cut it out, Henry!" I called.

"Cut what out?"

asked a voice behind me.

I turned around.

There stood Henry!

Yikes!

I looked back out the window.

Again the mummy wailed,

"I WANT MY GOLD!"

Then it ran off.

But now I saw something.

That mummy had on red sneakers.

I knew those red sneakers.

The mummy was Max!

Max and Henry were both

trying to trick me.

But why?

Henry said, "Hey, Jake.

Maybe you should give

the mummy your money."

Ah-ha!

Now I knew what Henry was up to!

This was all a trick to get my money!

I pretended to believe Henry.

"What should I do?" I asked.

Henry said, "Empty your bank.

Take all your money

to the theater tomorrow night.

Be there at eight o'clock.

Leave it by the door."

"Okay," I said.

"But will you and Max come with me?"

"Uh . . . I will," said Henry.

He looked nervous.

Then he added quickly,

"But we don't need Max."

The next day I called my Uncle Rob.

Uncle Rob is my dad's brother—

his <u>little</u> brother.

I knew he'd help me.

I told Uncle Rob about Henry's trick.

"Henry wants my money," I said.

"What do you want me to do?"

Uncle Rob asked.

I told him to dress up like a mummy.

A really gross mummy.

Then I told Uncle Rob where to go.

And what time to be there.

"Just make sure you really scare

Henry and Max,"

I told him.

Uncle Rob laughed and said,

"I will be there!"

NEXT ON
inside scoop:

MORE REPORTS ON
ESCAPED MUMMY

That night, Henry and I
walked to the theater.
I had all my money
in my backpack.
It was heavy.

"I am scared," I said.

Of course, I was just pretending!

I handed Henry my money.

"You go," I said.

Henry smiled.

"No problem," he said.

I watched Henry go.

Oh, boy!

I was going to get him now!

Henry stood and waited.

Pretty soon, along came Max—

Max the mummy.

This time I saw his red sneakers

<u>and</u> the bottoms of his jeans.

Henry pretended to be scared.

But he didn't pretend for long.

All of a sudden,

Uncle Rob shuffled out

from behind the theater.

Did he ever look disgusting!

His bandages were peeling off.

His skin looked like old oatmeal.

He held out his hands,

as if he wanted to choke Henry.

"I WANT MY GOLD!"

Uncle Rob wailed.

Henry and Max took one look at him.

"Ahhhhh!" they both cried.

Henry dropped the money.

He and Max ran away.

They never looked back.

I ran out from behind the bushes.

"Wow! You were great!" I cried.

I shook Uncle Rob's hand.

Ugh! It felt all mushy.

And did he ever stink!

"You look so real!" I told him.

I picked up my backpack.

Uncle Rob tried to grab it from me.

I jumped away.

"Oh, no!" I laughed.

"That was not part of the deal!"

"I WANT MY GOLD!"

said Uncle Rob.

Boy, he was <u>really</u> into this act!

Then he staggered off.

I thought he must want

to take off that yucky costume.

When I got home,

Henry and Max

were not there.

I was all alone.

The light was blinking

on our phone machine.

I pressed a button.

"Hi, Jake,"

said Uncle Rob's voice.

"I am really sorry

I could not make it tonight.

Something came up at work.

How about tomorrow night?

Give me a call."

What was going on?

My head was spinning.

Uncle Rob

had not come!

And if that other mummy

was not Uncle Rob . . .

and was not Henry . . .

and was not Max . . .

. . . then who was it?